First and foremost, I would like to ᵗ
and for creating us without a spirit
would like to extend my utmost gra
husband and best friend CJ. Withou   ....ulu only be
daydreams. To my three remarkable sons and niece, Jesse, Derek,
Lucas and Sanaya, life would be so dull without the color and love
you all provide. Thank you for all your support. To every other person,
you know who you are, that pushed me along and edified me, thank
you. Last but not least, D.J. and A.K. thank you for taking my visions
and helping them come to fruition. I am forever grateful. God bless
you all.

N.B.

MRZ Publishing Group, 167 Route 6, Unit 388, Baldwin Place, NY 10505.
Email: Bookfriends@mrzpublishing.com

For further information go to:
www.mrzpublishinggroup.com

Library of Congress Cataloging-in-Publication Data

ISBN: 978-0-9961959-6-6

Printed in the U.S.A.

ARIEL

Written by Naomi Bowen

Illustrated by Anna Krapiva

It was a bright and sunny day in August when Charlotte and her husband, Atticus, got to the hospital. Charlotte looked at Atticus with love in her eyes and squeezed his hand, trying at the same time to remember to breathe.

He pushed her in a wheelchair to the maternity ward, where their best friends, Sam, Bee, and their husbands, were waiting for Charlotte's arrival.

A cheer sprang up when the elevator doors opened.

"I can't believe I'm finally going to meet this little girl!" Sam said excitedly.

Charlotte smiled and said, "Us neither!"

"Did you guys figure out a name yet?" Bee asked.

"We've prayed about it and have a few names in mind," Charlotte said, "but we want to meet her first! There's a lot in a name, you know. Our child will carry her name with her throughout her life, and it needs to remind her of who she truly is."

Charlotte and Atticus continued on to the nurse's station, while their friends stayed in the waiting room. Sam and Bee paced back and forth. They felt they were about to explode with anticipation!

They had all grown up together and attended the same church, but Charlotte had always been the first to do everything. She had finished college first, gotten married first, and so today was no different. This baby would be the first born among their circle of friends.

A few hours passed. Then, suddenly, Atticus bursts through the doors into the waiting room. With a flurry of excitement he said, *"She's here*...our baby girl has arrived!"

All of the friends cheered with joy for Atticus, Charlotte, and their newborn baby girl. They quickly began asking questions.

"What's her name?"

"How much does she weigh?"

"How is Charlotte doing?"

"Who does she look like?"

Atticus was overwhelmed by their warmth. "Come and meet her for yourselves!" he said, still excited as he hurried back to Charlotte's room.

Charlotte was beaming from ear to ear as her delighted friends respectfully crept into the room. She looked at her daughter, whom she had been carrying in her tummy for nine months, and smiled. "Ariel..." she said lovingly, "...her name is Ariel."

Atticus ran his hand over the top of Ariel's tiny, soft head. "It means *Lion of God*," he said with pride, then kissed Charlotte's and Ariel's cheeks, one after the other. "And, *boy*, do we know God has *big* plans for this little girl."

"*Aww*... it's perfect!" their friends said fondly.

Ariel was a strong, happy, and beautiful baby. Her face was round, and she had a teeny nose. Her skin was softer than a chenille blanket, and she smelled just like freshly baked treats from your favorite bakery. Her soft, brown, curly tendrils of hair with ash blonde streaks complemented her olive skin, and her wide hazel eyes - with a splotch of green in her left eye - sparkled like sunlight.

Ariel soon grew to be an active and joyous toddler who walked and talked early, amazing her parents in *so* many ways. She didn't cry a lot, but kept her parents on their toes with her thirst for adventure and exploration.

She would search around her room with her eyes for new and curious things, and in no time was able to lift her whole body up the side of her crib. Before they knew it, she was standing and babbling like a bird at sunrise.

Charlotte and Atticus made jokes about her being a lawyer someday, after they saw how she'd argue with her stuffed animals!

She had one very special plushy, a stuffed lion named Logos that was toffee-colored and had a sunburst-yellow mane. Logos slept alongside her every night.

Ariel grew up with the kind of family that is 'chosen'. Her mother and father's childhood friends from church were always there when Ariel needed them. They never hesitated to step in and were always willing to answer her questions or help her solve a problem.

It was a promise they made to each other at Ariel's dedication ceremony —"Someone will *always* be there to guide you along the way, Ariel!"

As the pastor spoke loving words over Ariel and paraded her around, Charlotte and Atticus held one another proudly and lovingly. "Will you guide Ariel in the ways of the Lord?" the Pastor asked them.

"Yes, we will!" said Charlotte and Atticus together.

The Pastor continued, "Today marks the beginning of a relationship between Ariel and God, and the two of you will be responsible for how she finds her way."

The Pastor finished with a prayer, and then they went on to celebrate. Ariel was blessed enough to have not one set of Godparents, but *two*! They and all of their friends were overjoyed that Charlotte and Atticus had decided to show Ariel the same upbringing that they all knew so well.

Ariel grew up fast and always knew exactly what she wanted, so much so that on her second birthday she received a shiny, golden crown dotted with gems as a present. Ariel loved it so much that she put on her crown first thing in the morning every day. Each day she wore it with pride, no matter what she was doing.

Every new experience was a challenge to Ariel, presenting new opportunities for her to become stronger. She was not afraid of getting hurt whenever she attempted to discover something new.

Even learning to ride a bike was a breeze for her, give or take a few bruises!

Being a little afraid of heights didn't stop her from climbing a tall tree while hanging her tongue out the side of her mouth, or swinging as high as she could when playing with her friends or cousins.

She was never one to back down from a problem, and she kept her parents busy by always asking for help with strategies or figuring out a solution for someone in need. Her parents were convinced she was meant to be royalty.

When Ariel wore her crown at the store, people would smile and ask, "*Aww*... are you Daddy's little princess?"

"Nope, I'm the daughter of a King!" she'd respond, to which the people would laugh, thinking she was *so* cute.

6

Ariel wore that crown *everywhere*. She wore it at the breakfast table, when she brushed her teeth, to the park, when she fed the birds, and even when she visited her friends.

In truth she tried to wear it in the bath *and* to bed, but that didn't always work out so well.

"Ariel, please take that crown off. You can't possibly sleep with it on," her mother said.

"But Momma, how will the people in my dreams know I'm the daughter of a King if I'm not wearing my crown?"

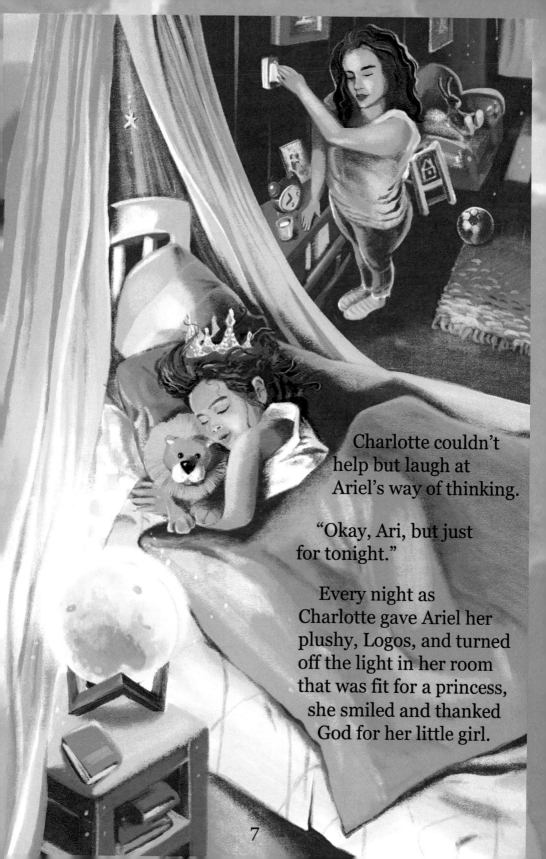

Charlotte couldn't help but laugh at Ariel's way of thinking.

"Okay, Ari, but just for tonight."

Every night as Charlotte gave Ariel her plushy, Logos, and turned off the light in her room that was fit for a princess, she smiled and thanked God for her little girl.

When Ariel was in
kindergarten, she met
a boy named Jesse.
Their friendship began when they were coloring.

Jesse dropped his crayon,and when he leaned down
to pick it up, his head rested on Ariel's elbow by accident.
Ariel was startled at first, but when Jesse looked up at her
with a nervous face, they both began to giggle. They
became inseparable from that day forward.

As Ariel grew older, she became even more fearless. When she played in her imagination, she'd slay giants and march in circles, breaking down city walls with her invisible trumpet.

"*Hey*, you're a girl - you can't do that kind of stuff!" the boys would say.

She would put her hands on her hips, lift her chin up, and then fire back, "I don't have to worry about what you say. I'm the daughter of a King, and I can do *anything*!"

One day at school during lunch, Ariel opened her Bumblebee lunch-box. "Yes!" she said excitedly, "Mom packed me mac-n'-cheese *and* a cupcake!" Ariel was about to dig in with glee, but quickly realized she'd forgotten something very important – to pray. She bowed her head, laced her fingers together, and began to pray like she always did.

"Dear Lord, thank you for this food. Bless it to my body, bless whoever made it, and please bless those who don't have any." She then popped open the lid of her turquoise thermos and dove into her yummy mac-n'-cheese.

Two boys, Luis and Christian, snickered behind her. She could clearly hear them talking about her. "Look at Ariel. She's casting a spell over her food again!" they said. "She's *so* weird."

Ariel looked over her shoulder but didn't say anything. Their comments made her feel a bit sad, but she didn't let it show. She couldn't understand why they were choosing to make fun of her.

After school she found Jesse and told him what happened. He stayed quiet, which was not really the response Ariel was hoping for. "Why aren't you saying anything, Jess?" Ariel asked.

"I don't know, Ari. I get that Luis and Christian were being mean but...I just think...well, if you didn't do all those *weird* things, maybe they wouldn't make fun of you."

Ariel was confused, but she chose to look for the right words to express her feelings.

"Jess, the things I do aren't *weird*. I pray before I eat because I am grateful that I have food. There are people in the world who don't even know when or where they will get their next meal."

Jesse didn't fully understand *why* she had to pray or say thank-you for her own food, but he agreed with Ariel about other people not having any.

One day at school, while Ariel and Jesse were playing tag, they noticed that Luis and Christian weren't playing together like they usually did. Ariel looked around the playground and soon saw Christian crying alongside the fence. She frowned and wondered what could have happened to make him cry all alone. Even though he often made fun of her, she felt like she needed to try to help him.

Ariel closed her eyes and prayed to herself, asking God to help her to help Christian. "Lord, it's Ariel again," she whispered. "I want to help Christian, but I need you to help me find the right words to use. Please, help me to listen. Help me to guide him in a way that is pleasing to you. Amen." She then turned and walked over to Christian.

"Where are you going, Ari?" Jesse asked.

"I'm going to see if Christian is okay," Ariel replied.

"Are you kidding? He's always so mean to you!"

Ariel knew that Jesse wouldn't understand, but she also knew she had the Lord's work to do.

Slowly she approached Christian. "Hey...Are you okay, Christian?"

Christian looked up to see who was talking to him. Seeing Ariel, he rolled his eyes, then turned away from her. "It's none of your business. I'm *fine*. Just get away from me, Ariel."

Ariel took a deep breath and stayed focused – she wasn't about to give up that easily. "I – I was just wondering why you aren't playing with Luis today. Is something wrong?"

"*Ugh...*" Christian sighed as he plucked a leaf from a weed that grew through the rubber playground floor. "It doesn't matter. It's not like you care anyway."

Ariel lowered her eyes and smiled softly. "But I *do* care. That's why I'm here talking with you."

Christian looked at her from the corner of his tear-filled eye.

"If you *must* know," he began reluctantly. "Luis thinks I stole his game cards. But I really didn't. Now he says he won't be my friend because I'm a thief." He crossed his arms in a huff and continued to look at the ground.

Ariel listened to his words and could see that Christian was deeply upset. "Well, I don't think you're a thief," she said.

Christian frowned, then quickly wiped his tears away, feeling a little embarrassed. "Why are you being so nice to me? I'm always teasing you – I thought you didn't even like me?"

"I understand." Ariel smiled. "But I'm the daughter of a King, and he told me to love everyone... even when they feel they may not deserve it."

Christian was suspicious, but he liked what Ariel was saying.

Having caught his attention now, Ariel started to tell Christian some pretty funny jokes. It didn't take long before he began laughing and agreed to walk with Ariel back to where Jesse was waiting.

Jesse looked at Ariel with a raised eyebrow as if to say, *What are you doing?*

Christian understood Jesse's facial expression. "Hey, Jesse. I know I can be mean sometimes. Ariel has forgiven and accepted me...I hope you can do the same?" He then saw a ball to his left and gently nudged it over to Jesse with his foot. "Can we maybe play together?"

Jesse was hesitant. But seeing the accepting smile in Ariel's eyes, he sighed and said, "Yeah, okay."

When they got back to class, Ariel knew that she would need to help Luis, too. His friendship with Christian had been messed up by a misunderstanding, and it was up to her to fix it.

"Luis?" Ariel began.

"What do you want, Ariel?" Luis replied a little bitterly.

"Christian told me that you think he stole your game cards. He said he really didn't, though, and I believe him. Can you think of any reason why your best friend would do that?" Ariel asked.

Luis thought about it for a moment. While he hadn't found his game cards anywhere, in truth he was missing his best friend more. The more he thought about it, the more he realized that Christian would never take anything that didn't belong to him.

He looked at Christian. "So, you're saying you really didn't take my cards?"

"I would *never* do that to you, Luis!" Christian replied sincerely. "You're my best friend!"

Luis frowned, feeling a little bad. "I - I'm really sorry I accused you, Christian."

"It's okay," Christian said. "I know you were just upset… and I know those cards mean a lot to you."

A smile formed in the corner of Luis's mouth. "Do – do you have time to help me look for them?"

"Of course!" said Christian, delighted that he and Luis had managed to overcome their misunderstanding. He then said to Ariel, "Hey, I just want to say thank-you for helping us today."

He scratched his head as he added, "You really didn't *have* to. I probably wouldn't have helped me if I was you."

Ariel sighed, then laughed. "It's a good thing I'm not you then! I saw you were in need, and I just wanted to help. I'm glad it worked out!"

And with that, Christian and Luis began to search the classroom for the game cards. Ariel was pleased she'd been guided to help them in the best way possible.

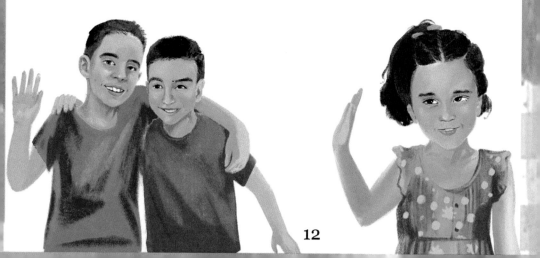

As Ariel grew into a teenager, her crown didn't quite fit anymore. However, she still had Logos and could rely on him for company at night.

Like all teenagers, she went through a few trials and tribulations, but always with a smile. When she didn't make the softball team or the drama club, she didn't blame anyone or anything.

Instead, she believed that God had a reason for her not being a part of either, and that He had an even more special place for her somewhere else.

Like when she made it onto Varsity Cheer in her freshman year, or when she and her friend Ella started a Bible-journaling club.

When others were stressed about tests and relationships, she prayed instead. In her heart she knew she was still royalty, and she did not have the fear that a lot of her friends had.

Ariel and Jesse remained best friends, of course. As they grew older together, they learned to lean on each other when times got tough. They would often talk about the girls Jesse liked and the boys Ariel liked, while studying in Ariel's backyard. Every now and again, Jesse would become quite emotional when a girl he liked did not feel the same way about him.

"Jess, she just wasn't the best girl for you," Ariel would explain with empathy. "You obviously deserve better, and I know God has the perfect fit for you out there."

Jesse never quite understood what she meant. He would continue to look at the pages in his textbooks and mumble, just loud enough for Ariel to hear, "You keep saying that, but *when* am I going to meet her?"

Ariel would usually laugh and say, "When God wants you to... *duh*!"

Jesse would roll his eyes and squeeze out a smile. "And how about you? Has God made a match for you?"

"I don't know yet. I'm still young. But I pray for the right boyfriend in time, and I just *know* he's going to be amazing because he's going to love Jesus!" She smiled at the thought. "I'm the daughter of a King, remember - only the best for this princess!" Ariel always knew in her heart that God would light her path.

She grew into a young adult, bold and confident but in a different way – as though she was a light in the dark. She would help others study for tests between classes, in most cases going out of her way for anyone in need.

Even when people made fun of her, she would smile. She knew God had her back. Although forgiving is a hard thing for many people to do, forgiveness was something deeply embedded in her nature.

Jesse often asked, "How do you always stay so calm even when things get really bad?"

"I'm the daughter of a King," she replied. "You should know that by now!"

Jesse shrugged his shoulders and sighed. He knew that she was raised differently, and because of this, he didn't always understand her ways.

One day, while they were sitting in Ariel's yard by the pool, listening to music like they often did on the weekends, Jesse suddenly jumped as he looked at his watch. "Ari, it's 11:11 a.m. – the universe is listening, *make a wish!*"

Ariel replied with a knowing chuckle. "Oh, Jess – I don't do that stuff. I'd rather pray!" She lowered her sunglasses and looked over the top of them. "Better results, you know!"

"Why do you always pray so much?" Jesse asked. "Aren't you only supposed to pray when you need something?" He frowned. "I've prayed a few times, but nothing's happened."

"What did you pray about, Jess?" Ariel asked, leaning toward him. "I don't really want to talk about it," Jesse muttered. He didn't really like to speak about his feelings much. Rather, he was a good listener and prided himself on that.

"*C'mon*, Jess, I want to help if I can. Do you pray for the fighting to stop between your parents? I can hear them arguing when we're on the phone sometimes."

Jesse tried to change the subject. "I'm fine..." he looked at his watch again "I have to go home now anyway."

As he left, in a bit of a hurry, Ariel could not help but feel concerned about his worrisome behavior. That night she knelt by her bed and prayed.

"Lord, I don't know exactly what Jesse needs. But you do, God. You know *everything* that goes on. Please help him to get through whatever he is going through. Thank you so much for this life and for everything you do for me daily. Amen."

And with that she pulled Logos toward her chest and went to sleep.

Toward the end of the following week at school, Ariel could tell that Jesse was growing more upset. He hadn't even opened his Blue-Ranch Doritos and Coke that he usually couldn't wait to enjoy every day during recess.

"Jess, I'm no fool. I can tell there's something bothering you. Please tell me - what's going on?" Ariel asked.

While Jesse had avoided such questions before, this time he looked at Ariel and started pouring his heart out to her.

"Ari, my parents fight *every* day. They keep putting me in the middle of their arguments, too, and make me choose between them." He cringed at the thought. "I just – I just wish I could... *move away*! I even tried praying like you said... but *nothing ever* changes!"

Ariel felt his pain. "Jess"—she touched his hand with hers—"I didn't know it was that bad. I just figured all parents fight sometimes." There was silence for a moment, and then she slid the Doritos across the table with a sympathetic smile.

He couldn't hold his feelings inside anymore. He put his head down and fought back the tears.

Ariel held his hand. "I'm deeply sorry you're going through this, Jess. There's a youth group at my church every Friday night – tonight. Do you want to join me? I know you've said 'no' before, but it'll take your mind off of the things going on at home."

Jesse was hesitant at first, but then he gave it some thought. "You know, Ari, anywhere is better than home right now."

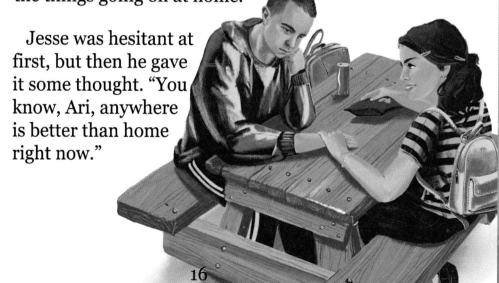

After school, Jesse went home with Ariel. It was always calm and warm there with a sense of peace, a homey feeling he did not get to experience very often. They had big, comfy couches for watching movies or for taking an afternoon nap. All of the rooms were colorful, and the walls were covered with photos and paintings of special memories. There was even a picture of Jesse and Ariel at her Luau ninth birthday party hanging in the hallway. In Ariel's home no one fought with or blamed him for anything. He truly liked being there.

Ariel's Mom, Charlotte, had made spaghetti and meatballs for dinner. As they sat down to eat, they took each other's hands and lowered their heads to pray. In truth, Jesse always felt a little weird doing this with them, but this time he joined in.

During dinner they laughed and talked about everyone's day. Charlotte put another meatball on Jesse's plate. "So, Jess," she said, "what's new with you?"

"Nothing much, Missus C," Jesse replied. " I am thankful for you having me over for dinner, though."

Atticus, Ariel's Dad, smiled and said, "Jess, you practically live here!"

Jesse felt a little embarrassed. "I know. I'm – I'm sorry. I don't mean to impose..."

Atticus and Charlotte quickly sat up in their chairs. "Stop that, Jess! Goodness, we love you as though you were our own. You're Ariel's best friend in the *whole* world, and you're *always* welcome here. Don't you ever forget that, okay?"

Jesse looked down at his plate. A teeny tear formed in his eye. He felt *so* much strength and warmth from what they'd said. It opened his heart to what felt like soft rays of morning sunlight, and he couldn't help but smile.

Once dinner was done, it was time for youth group. Of course, it was Jesse's first time.

17

After the newcomers were introduced, Pastor Rick read a few scriptures from the Bible. He spoke about faith, telling everyone that if they prayed with their whole heart every day, God would do infinitely more than whatever it is they might ask for.

At one point, Jesse felt as if Pastor Rick was talking directly to him. He began to think about his parents, his life, and how Ariel always handled circumstances and issues so well.

Ariel then introduced Jesse to her circle of youth-group friends - Ella, Anna, Wes and Asher. They were happy to meet him and, for the time that followed, all they did was talk about God, play games, and sing in worship.

Towards the end, Jesse's smile was stretching from ear to ear. "You know, at the start I didn't think I would enjoy this..." he said.

"But you did?" asked Ariel.

"Yeah." Jesse laughed a little inside. "I can't explain it... but it feels like I'm really meant to be here tonight."

"Of course you are!" Ariel said, with the others in agreement. "God has a way of making things happen, but only when the time is right!"

Jesse went home that night feeling something he couldn't find the words to describe. He didn't know what it was, but he knew he'd never felt it before. He lay in his bed and began thinking as he shuffled through the pages of a Bible that Ariel had given him a few years before.

"Faith..." he mumbled. "I wonder... If I have enough faith and choose to pray daily, will I *really* get what my heart desires?"

A couple of days passed. At school Ariel began to recognize a notable difference in Jesse's behavior.

For some reason, he was asking her a lot of questions about faith and prayer.

During lunch, as they sat on the green-turf field, he asked her, "Okay, so...how do you *get* faith? When are we *supposed* to pray...and do we have to say certain words, or can we say whatever we want to?"

Ariel giggled a little. "Jess"—she rubbed his arm quickly - "faith is not something you can *get*. It's not a thing, it's a feeling. Faith is like hope. It's something you have to *want* to feel. Through all the bad things, *faith* is believing that something good *will* come, even if you can't see it and don't know when. Then you just have to get on with your life, constantly knowing that it will eventually come - if it is God's will, that is. If what you're asking for is not meant for you, you can be thankful for it not coming your way, as it simply wasn't part of God's plan for you."

She pulled her turkey-and-cheese sandwich from her lunchbox. "And, yeah, we can speak with and pray to God whenever we want! He's *always* listening. It's pretty awesome! You see, we are the children of God, the almighty King..." She paused, then looked him right in the eye, "...and that includes *you*! When we're fighting battles, He strengthens us. When we begin to feel alone, we only need to remember that He is right here with us. My mom has told me, since I was a little girl, that my name means *Lion of God*. How can I be worried when I know God *made* me to be strong?"

At home that night Jesse started to pray — he prayed with all the attention and intention he had to give. He had tried before, but not with as much conviction as he had now. This time he was finding faith to be something that was worth believing in. He had found the feeling called 'hope'.

"God, I really need help. Even though I've tried really hard, I can't get my parents to stop fighting. Please help them — please help me to help them."

He paused once he was done with his request. He thanked God for listening then remembered there was a special word that Ariel always used to say thank-you to God. He tapped his finger on his forehead, trying to remember it...

"Oh, *yes*! That's it — Amen!"

Ariel and Jesse grew closer and closer still over the next few weeks. He felt he could trust her now more than ever. The Friday night youth-group meetings became their favorite thing to do together. Jesse also joined Ariel in her bible-journaling club that she'd started long ago with her friend, Ella.

Each day Jesse's smile showed just how excited he was to be experiencing a relationship with God, more and more, in his daily life. He even began to hold hands and pray with Ariel and Ella at lunch at school, no matter the funny looks others would give them. All Jesse could do was hope that they, too, would find faith in their lives one day.

One morning Jesse ran up to Ariel at the school's entrance. He'd been waiting for her to arrive, as he had some awesome news to share with her. He hugged her so tightly and then lifted her right off the ground, swinging her around in sheer joy.

"Ariel laughed, feeling giddy, "Jess! It's *way* too early for all this excitement! Tell me, my friend, what have you been blessed with, because clearly that's what's happened!"

"*Ariel*," he said so loudly that it sounded as though he was shouting, "He's *real*!"

"Who's real?" Ariel said, even though she had a feeling she knew exactly who he was talking about.

"God," he yelled, "He *is* real! I've been praying for a little while now and it made me feel good, but nothing was really changing at home. All of a sudden, last night, my parents came into my room and sat me down, telling me they were sorry. Sorry for all the fighting and sorry for blaming me… and then they said that they are going to get counseling. They really want their marriage to work. We're going to be a family again!"

Ariel smiled, almost in tears. Without thinking she began a prayer. "Dear God, I *know* that was you!" she whispered with eyes closed, her smile beaming up to the sky. "Thank you!" She then looked at Jesse and hugged him tightly. "Jess, that's the best news *ever*! I am so, *so* happy for you!"

As they looked into each other's eyes, simultaneously they said, "God is *so* good!"

When Ariel went home that day, she couldn't stop smiling. Prayers had been answered like a miracle, and she had to record the event by journaling something special in her Bible. This way, in times of doubt, she could always look back at the moment and remember that there was still much goodness in the world, when God was put in charge.

She jumped onto her bed with her pen in her mouth and reached for her Bible on her bedside table. She turned to *2 Timothy 1:7* and wrote what she read - *For God gave us a spirit not of fear but of power and love and self-control.*

Alongside it she wrote her own creative note in calligraphy – *Faith over fear.* She decorated the whole page with tiny detailed and pretty flowers surrounding the words she had written, as a way to make them really stand out. They were important words, after all, and needed a beautiful background to support them.

As she closed her Bible after an hour of decorating, she held it to her chest, then looked out of her bedroom window at the wonderful day outside. "God, I *know* that you are in control," she said, "and for that I am extremely grateful."

Time after time, as Ariel grew to be a strong, nurturing, and helpful woman, all of her prayers were answered in just the right ways.

She never questioned *how* they were answered, understanding that God has His own way of doing things. She learned not to assume the exact *way* God would help her. All she knew was that he always would.

Ariel *knew,* every minute of every day, that she was *never* alone. She believed in God's eternal promise and knew that as long as she continued to trust Him she would *always* be okay.

This trust, and the strength of her faith, was the reason for her name – *Lion of God.*

The End

Made in the USA
Middletown, DE
24 December 2020